LOCAL MEN

Also by James Whitehead

JOINER (a novel)

DOMAINS (poems)

LOCAL MEN

Poems by
JAMES WHITEHEAD

UNIVERSITY OF ILLINOIS PRESS
Urbana   Chicago   London

LIBRARY OF CONGRESS CATALOGING IN PUBLICATION DATA

Whitehead, James.
  Local men.

  I. Title.
PS3573.H48L6   811'.5'4   79–10660
ISBN 0–252–00763–8
ISBN 0–252–00764–6 pbk.

ACKNOWLEDGMENTS

These poems—several in somewhat different form—were first published in the following periodicals: *The Back Door:* "Long Tour: The Country Music Star Explains Why He Put Off the Bus and Fired a Good Lead Guitar in West Texas"; *Barataria Review:* "I Write in a Peculiar Mood Unworthy of the Trust," "A Better Than Average Boy Reconsiders the Fact That His Momma Taught Him Right from Wrong," "The Travelling Picker's Prayer and Dream"; *Books: A New Orleans Review:* "He Remembers How He Didn't Understand What Lieutenant Dawson Meant"; *Concerning Poetry:* "Nonce Sonnet as Epistle—A Local Man Begins to Understand Why He and His Friend Failed to Crash and Burn with the Good Women They Encountered in a Distant Town"; *December:* "The Plain Story of Macintosh the White Cropper Who Never Stopped Talking Until He Got to Death"; *The Denver Quarterly:* "He Records a Little Song for a Smoking Girl," "The Narrative Hooper and L.D.O. Sestina with a Long Last Line"; *The Film Journal:* "A Brief Review of *The Devils*"; *The Greensboro Review:* "A Local Man Doesn't Like the Music," "He Loves the Trailer Park and Suffers Telling Why"; *The Hollins Critic:* "A Local Man Remembers Betty Fuller," "After Reading *Beowulf* Again"; *Jeopardy:* "The Delta Chancery Judge After Reading *Aubrey's Brief Lives*"; *The Little Review:* "For Berryman," "For Gen," "In Neshoba County"; *Mississippi Review:* "The Recently Sober Man's Prayer for Autumn"; *The New Orleans Review:* "For Our Fifteenth Anniversary"; *Poetry Now:* "A Local Man Can't Handle the Lady's Problems," "After Having Read Aloud Some Favorite Poems the Local Circuit Judge Enjoys Fine Table Whiskey and High Talk," "Dealing With Mary Fletcher," "Good Linemen Live in a Closed World," "The Leflore County Lawyer Recollects His Client Sullivan," "The Curious Local Banker After Having Read a Recent Anthology," "Troubled in a Dallas Hotel Room He Remembers Lady Years Later," "Trying to Explain a Bad Man to a Good Man at the Neshoba County Fair in 1971," "Visionary Oklahoma Sunday Beer," "Wherein the Lawyer from George

County Recounts Events Soon and Some Time After He Crossed the Bar"; *Poetry Texas:* "A Recently Recorded Picker Experiences a Complicated Sadness and Provokes Himself into a Prayer," "Pay Attention, Son"; *Quarterly West:* "A Local Man Ponders a Letter He Has Received from a Liberal Woman He Continues to Admire"; *Raven:* "A Better Than Average Boy Prays After Loving the Afflicted Daughter and Wife"; *Shenandoah:* "He Remembers Something from the War"; *Southern Poetry Review:* "About a Year After He Got Married He Would Sit Alone in an Abandoned Shack in a Cotton Field Enjoying Himself," "He Remembers Figuring a Logic for the Life That Went On the Summers He Cruised Timber," "The Alabama Man Remembers All He Can About the Battered Children and the Woman With Almost Perfect Skin in Mobile Seven Years Ago," "The Country Music Star Begins His Politics," "What the Chancery Judge Told the Young Lawyer After a Long Day in Court"; *The Southern Review:* "A Local Contractor Flees His Winter Trouble and Saves Some Lives in a Knoxville Motel Room," "Doing Bidness," "Having Gained Some Spiritual Ruthlessness but Still Confused by What Has Happened a Local Man Considers a Friend Who Died Alone," "He Listens to His Brother Begin to Enjoy a Beautiful Social Woman at a Party," "His Slightly Longer Story Song," "Some Better Than Average Advice About Writing from the Elder Local Novelist Who Is a Craftsman of Sorts and Wise and Prolific," "Some Local Men After Their Election"; *Southern Voices:* "On Finding Her Out When He Comes In, Their Children Fast Asleep After the Holiday Is Over"; *Strivers' Row:* "A Local Man Is Drunk but Under Control in a Tonk with Marginal Friends"; *The Vanderbilt Poetry Review:* "A Local Man Estimates What He Did for His Brother Who Became a Poet and What His Brother Did for Him."

FOR JACK MARR
GLENN RAY
AND TOM ROYALS —
AND FOR MY BROTHER, JERRY WHITEHEAD

Lord, if I judge 'em
Let me give 'em lots of room—
Tom T. Hall

With this I do not mean to propose
a peace treaty—
Emma Goldman

There is a disease of the human mind,
called the metaphysical tendency, that
causes man, after he has by logical
process abstracted the quality from
an object, to be subject to a kind
of hallucination that makes him take
the abstraction for the real thing—

Errico Malatesta

CONTENTS

LOCAL MEN

A LOCAL MAN REMEMBERS BETTY FULLER

Betty Fuller cried and said, Hit me.
I did. Which made her good and passionate
But Betty Fuller never came. Fate
Decreed that Betty Fuller would not see
The generosity a lively house
And loyal husband bring. She lost her mind
In Mendenhall. She got herself defined
As absolutely mad. A single mouse
Caused her to run exactly down the line
Of a wide road, running both north and south
With execrations pouring from her mouth.

She's out at Whitfield doing crazy time
And she can't possibly remember me
Among the rest. I'm satisfied she can't.

THE PLAIN STORY OF MACINTOSH THE WHITE CROPPER WHO NEVER STOPPED TALKING UNTIL HE GOT TO DEATH

By the time he quit talking and got to death
His eyes were clabbered and the Picayunes
Had scoured down his lungs and throat and nose—
He hardly had a sense left except for sound
To hear his own voice with.
He'd bellow, "To hell with it—noise and feel
Is all the humans need,"
And then he'd squeal and dig at his open fly.

The loud delight of hearing his cruelties
And venialities
Come back around his yard in raunchy circles—
Cat screams, rooster crows
And bitch howls—like all
The generations of animals he'd kept
And buried—was what he lived on mostly.
He chanted those fine incestuous memories
To anyone who got within earshot—
Someone a half mile down the road could hear
Himself addressed before he saw the old man
Boiling off through the heat
Alive with Macintosh's history—
In broad sunshine a voice more furious
For ears than brigades of Turks—
A redneck Odyssey afloat on air
Like brigantines across a wild catarrh—
A voice fired through light like Minié balls or flak . . .

Children walking the far ridge could hear the time
He won a hundred on a doped horse in Memphis
And how he lost it on the best damned rut
A single man can get
And worth the Yellow Dog—

You'd see him blindly pissing off his porch
And know he did it through the floor inside.
No way in the world to make his going pleasant,
Though finally his yelling did stop. He fell
From his steps the time
I was close enough to cheer on his story
That celebrated how he'd killed a neighbor's brother
For riding a colt to death—and the whole white sky
Was mad as hell to see it, the breaking down
Of anything as ravenous and mean as Macintosh.

Weeds grew up through the floor and reached the ceiling.
His shack filled up with humid foliage
And then collapsed into a green
That dominates the fields for miles.
Sawgrass and dock and bitterweed
Reek eyeless in the heat
And down the road the silences are eloquent.

IN NESHOBA COUNTY

He shoots his snooker standing straight up
Because he can't bend—poke shots
And mostly they're inaccurate—
But when one does work
It shakes the pocket
And shivers the fat he is sunk in.

God, how his trousers ride up his huge ass
And how his mother must have loved on him.

His pale skin bulges over his high-top shoes—
It is whiter even
Than his rolled down
Sheer socks that have red veins
Like blood with poison in it.
Because of politics I fear this man's pain.

AFTER READING *BEOWULF* AGAIN

How shall we bear the fury of this dream?

The Rose of Heaven is nowhere seen. No Devil
Builds the Fancy City. The creatures seem,
However terrible, the easy drivel
Shot from Sunday sets. In fact, they seem

From Disneyland—our mothers' eyes that swear
On sex—our fathers' honest hands that scream
Above our butts. Sorrow is everywhere
And the goddamned story is told in starts and fits

As if a man's whole life were simply fights—
Redneck Jocastas, Dragon Bankers, Tits
Gunning for Glory in the name of Sense. Nights!
The only light being devouring bad breath.

How shall we tolerate this human death?

ABOUT A YEAR AFTER HE GOT MARRIED
HE WOULD SIT ALONE IN AN ABANDONED SHACK
IN A COTTON FIELD ENJOYING HIMSELF

I'd sit inside the abandoned shack all morning
Being sensitive, a fair thing to do
At twenty-three, my first son born, and burning
To get my wife again. The world was new
And I was nervous and wonderfully depressed.

The light on the cotton flowers and the child
Asleep at home was marvelous and blessed,
And the dust in the abandoned air was mild
As sentimental poverty. I'd scan
Or draw the ragged wall the morning long.

Newspaper for wallpaper sang but didn't mean.
Hard thoughts of justice were beyond my ken.
Lord, forgive young men their gentle pain,
Then bring them stones. Bring their play to ruin.

HE REMEMBERS FIGURING A LOGIC
FOR THE LIFE THAT WENT ON THE SUMMERS
HE CRUISED TIMBER

One time a wildcat jumped from a tree, and once
We saw twelve snakes in a single day of work,
But mostly there was little more than the dance
Of flying insects on the sun—then back
To Woodville for a sorry meal and beer
And waitresses who loved the picture show
And probably a screw without much cheer.
I tried to understand what I should know.

I thought of phrases. *Natural weather* was one.
A slow mean life was another. Also *bad taste*.

Late at night the sun stayed on my skin
And the motel sheets were stiff, and my smoke was a waste
Unless by force of mind I figured breath
Goes back to the leaves, rounding out my death.

THE DELTA CHANCERY JUDGE
AFTER READING *AUBREY'S BRIEF LIVES*

1
I think of shame, embarrassment and crime

Rott with the rotten;
Let the dead bury the dead
And that for William Chillingworth, Divine,
Because he mostly died of syphylis.
I agree with Aubrey—
Dr. Cheynell was unkind to Chillingworth.

Old John Aubrey was a man of parts
And was a sot: *Sot that I am,* he often wrote.

2
All that rancor, all that plague and fire
And every reputation cheap as lice—
It boggles me the sort of life I know.

"As he laye unravelling in the agonie of death,
the Standers-by could hear him say softly,
I have seen the Glories of the world"—
Isaac Barrow was that decent man.

Moniti meliora We now have better counsel—
How I doubt that sentence!

3
Last week I fixed divorce for three young men
And each was wrong
Unworldly and unkind to his desperate wife.
Dumb as pig shit, each was terrified
Of anything his mother didn't know.

Our simple education softens teeth
And all their fathers bit their thickened tongues.
Their children never will
Strap on or see the glories of the world.

4

Who is the King of Chancery today?
Who can personify Sweet Equity
Now everything begins with common law?

My court is for insurance men who lose
And give their money out of policy
Because I contradict my style and rule
Almost exclusively
Against their company.
I will be re-elected.

5

A year ago there was a funeral,
The mistress to a friend,
And when the graveside nervous prayer was done,
His wife let go a scream:
No one to keep the bastard off of me!

He was gone for fifteen weeks alone
But never more than eighty miles from here
Doing business from his motel rooms.
He got back home and there was no reprieve.

6
Sometimes my few good friends with their good wives
And I with mine, we leave
Denying every province of our pain
For days of games and plays.

Sots all, we will maintain some glory for this world.

Smoking all that much has got her eyes
Pinched and a little lined—so the misery
Of cigarettes deserves a song. Prize
For doing anything, catastrophe
In small doses, smoke cuts into a face
Almost as deep as Benzedrine and booze.

Still she's a lovely girl in every place
Because she is so young. O she will lose
Her surfaces of head in love and time
Though all the rest stay smooth and be close-pored.
Her legs would make a blind man smile, and rime—
Her belly and the thing in sweet accord
Years from now will cry, Forgive, forgive
My cigarettes, I swallowed smoke alive.

THE NARRATIVE HOOPER AND L.D.O. SESTINA
WITH A LONG LAST LINE
for Leon Stokesbury

One fall not far from Ozark, Arkansas
A gentle sheriff saw a hairy man
Upon the berm—hairy in the extreme
This man was, but kindly from his bearded face.
He hunkered there upon the fading grass
And to the sheriff seemed entirely at peace.

It's wonderful to see a boy at peace
So much he seems to love our Arkansas,
Even if he's vagrant on the grass,
The sheriff thought, who was a decent man,
Although not one to wear a bearded face,
Which faces were to him at least a bit extreme.

Could be this boy's entirely extreme,
A hooper flipped on dope and not at peace
At all with Arkansas—he'd have to face
This hairy one near Ozark, Arkansas
To prove the Law is not the lesser man
Than one who is so fearless in the autumn grass.

And so the sheriff stopped his car, on the grass
And on the berm, in a state of mind extreme
For such a gentle and a decent man
Who lived in fact essentially at peace
With every normal man in Arkansas.
He parked, but showed some fear upon his razored face.

It was a moment all good men will face
In time, and man to man, on God's own grass—
We all must be in Ozark, Arkansas
Or somewhere just the same and as extreme
Some time, attempting to maintain the peace,
As honest sheriff or as gentle hairy man.

And so it was with our two friends. The man
Who had the hair on said, "Sheriff, your face
Suggests I've done some thing to break the peace
While taking of my ease upon the grass."
"I'm not exactly sure it's that extreme . . .
Are you a hooper?" the sheriff mumbled, then clearly saw

His man was nervous—"Boy, are you on grass
Or L.D.O.!" His face was now extreme.
"Peace, Sheriff," said the hairy man, "I'm no hooper—I'm
    from Dumas, Arkansas."

HE REMEMBERS SOMETHING FROM THE WAR

In Kansas during the war
    my grandfather made a big thing
    of a car left out in our alley—
There's bullet holes and human blood
    so hurry up and eat your supper.
And the whole world would jiggle a little
    like Jello, when he was nervous.
Mother and grandmother were gone
    to the movies to see my father winning
    the war in Europe—grandfather
    never went to the movies or church
    and for the same reasons.
This is a lot like the real trouble
    your father is having in Germany,
    he said, as we walked past our victory garden
    then down our alley.

The things themselves were plain—
    a blue Nash and a windbreaker
    stiff with blood
    but I wasn't scared
    even by the stain itself
    until he told the story
    about how for some reason
    a hitch-hiker had murdered a farmer
    then left the car and jacket in our alley
    after dumping out the dead farmer
    in the woods of northern Arkansas.
About the time the police arrived
    I asked why in our alley?
He was the only father I had
    those long years during the war
    my mother was gone to in the movies.

Later that night mother and grandmother
    scolded him for getting drunk
    because they didn't know the things
    behind the garden
    and wouldn't until the morning news
    that told another story
    which was a lie grandfather said,
    like Roosevelt.
Upstairs he staggered near the door
    outside my room and close to my bed
    where that night in a sweaty dream
    I saw a German soldier
    catching a ride
    with my own father
    in my own father's M-4 tank
    that was standing out in our alley.

THE RECENTLY SOBER MAN'S PRAYER FOR AUTUMN

Send a cool day, Lord, and let me rest—let wind
Blow hard and the rain cease. My insect life
All summer long is rich and full. Offend
Their wings away. Sober as a butter knife
Please let me be, and that for morning bread.

A patient decency is what I want—
Much more chattering and I am dead.
Lord, am I bitten into sense, or bent?

Unlike nice birds they fly backwards, hover
Like helicopters. They don't pace so well
As geese or albatrosses. I'm no lover!
Drive insects down some sea! Diminish hell.
Strictly speaking, Lord, I live in fear.

I shudder as your beast and breathe fresh air.

A BETTER THAN AVERAGE BOY PRAYS
AFTER LOVING THE AFFLICTED DAUGHTER AND WIFE

Lord, the will to make small virtue stand!
Lord, my fear of her husband and father. Lord,
Those two incapable of her. My hand
Passed over her afflictions where were stored
The sadness and the need. Did I do right
Or cunningly or cruelly or wrong?

I have strange dreams wherein I have to mount
The bent creation—and there is a song
Whose bars sing harmony except one line
In the language of a keen of small pleasure.
She said, Thank you—I think that was just fine.

Husband and father will never measure
What she knows. Don't you agree? I want
Some peace in this. Please curse the ones who won't.

DOING BIDNESS
for William Harrison

Encourage the several small catastrophes
You suffer every day, especially
Abuse over the phone. Smile. Say cheese
While they are crying, Bastard! Shit! I see
Your point. Say that you see something, a point.

Outside small mountains exhale and the dead are warm,
Locked down in heavy August, don't worry rent.
Masts pop over the verge, pray for a storm
With organ music. Steerage is yourself.
The worst is yet to come. The phonecalls aren't.

Just one one day will stutter toward a laugh,
Alive within your office, forefinger bent
Against the trigger. Well, the round won't kill.
But, Christ, the noise, the noise is terrible.

NONCE SONNET AS EPISTLE—A LOCAL MAN BEGINS TO UNDERSTAND WHY HE AND HIS FRIEND FAILED TO CRASH AND BURN WITH THE GOOD WOMEN THEY ENCOUNTERED IN A DISTANT TOWN

You said the smart ones do it right away—
Even quicker than the dumb—but ours
Were in the middle distances, good girls
With normal minds and common debts to pay—
Rents and children in the second room,
Divorce and separation in their dreams—
No way, no way—and when that baby screams
You know the earth took more than a single day.

Why'd their husbands leave with them so warm?
Neither one would turn a good man down
Or deny the sensual request
If it's sincere. They do their decent best
And like it, too. Somebody did them harm
Then ran. A balanced woman requires charm.

A LOCAL MAN IS DRUNK BUT UNDER CONTROL
IN A TONK WITH MARGINAL FRIENDS

Her eyes are slightly clouded and sleepy dirt
Is up against her pitted nose on both sides
And her sour yellow mess has not been brushed
The hundred strokes that every lady knows—
It hangs down over her shoulders in coils
And her skin is like a baked potato peel's
Insides. I know
The man she's nourishing. He says he loves
The way she smells and when he gets drunk a little
He goes insane over how his woman is.

Lord, their nervousness—
Any Quaker's hour would be heaven to them—
Every man
With discipline and work to take pride in
Drives the bottle down his tender throat.
These skinny lovers in their bed make sounds
Exactly like Ezekiel's bones, but they,
Unlike the ancient vision, can't get up.
Their house I went to once is like a pen,
Sour mash and pork and sour grain.

Nothing takes shape here.
They only care for me because I pay . . .
They hate me for my pleasures in the rain
On nights I come to town . . .
They hate the easy horses of my dreams
And everything that goes
With children and money and a fancy wife.
Both have said I lead the easy life—
And there is no Christ of Gin to save them with
And God's own politics would be too late.

GOOD LINEMEN LIVE IN A CLOSED WORLD

Good linemen live in a closed world—they move
Inside themselves to move themselves against
The others and their violence—they give
To interior visions whole seasons no good sense
Would approve—their insides creak and groan, crying
A thing that's trapped along the line is shrill
And curious and wants out. Bodies playing
Laugh and dream to gain the massive will
Their trade requires. These men maintain, they attack,
They suffer repetition for years and years.
Part war and similar to art, their work
Is sometimes elegant. Inside their fears
At the closed center of one fear, they move
Quickly against themselves with a massive love.

ON FINDING HER OUT WHEN HE COMES IN, THEIR CHILDREN FAST ASLEEP AFTER THE HOLIDAY IS OVER

No way. No way. There's no reasoning
How conjugal the terrors are, the rage
These women feel against their men. The thing
Is gone. Old marriage like the persiflage

Of maiden aunts on dope is strictly mad.
We men grow facial hair for war again,
Repeating like Edwardians, Cad, Cad,
Emitting awful tropes that merely grin
Like the face she drew in the pumpkin pie.

I jog these rhythms in a dream, praying
Not to scream at her again, or cry,
Asking why my drunk tongue keeps dully saying
Not even children sleeping well are worth this,
And why no grace should make bad lovers kiss.

HE REMEMBERS HOW HE DIDN'T UNDERSTAND
WHAT LIEUTENANT DAWSON MEANT

Lieutenant Dawson said he'd known the girl
For fifteen years
But I couldn't read his face
Or his shaved head—
He said there's something cruel
About the way these people live—Disgrace
And Violence and Crime.
He made a list
That never added up to heavy grief.
Three times he opened up then closed a fist
And said he'd known she'd never have a life.

Outside the small and mean low-ceilinged room
Where she lay dead, her pretty body torn
And ruined by the shoe and stolen ring
Her boyfriend used,
Dawson freed a groan
That wasn't clearly out of sympathy—
Then said this is your basic tragedy.

A LOCAL MAN DOESN'T LIKE THE MUSIC

Those tunes don't recollect one memory
I ever had. Not one could call my name.
And when the music isn't company
It's time to go and time to change your mind.

I've been dissatisfied. My pretty wives
Were decent, warm, and wrong. My sons have played
It smarter than I did. My daughters' lives
Are better than their mothers'. They are good.

I love them all, but I don't love them well.
I've been dissatisfied to be alone,
The one sure way to make your bed in hell.

I'll change my mind. I'll like to where I've gone,
Whatever trailer park or motel room.
Alone or with some girl, I'll write a song.

HE LOVES THE TRAILER PARK AND SUFFERS
TELLING WHY

A hopeful life is possible out here,
And sometimes nervous,
Though few of us will ever travel much.
Storms are what we fear.
Sometimes our metal homes are worse than thatch
Or mud huts or hide tents, when the wind comes.
Trailer Park Destroyed—a common line
Because nobody ever ties them down
The way suggested.

That's hopeful, true, a sign
Of basic piety, unworldliness
To help define the insane goings-on
You read about. Lives here are quite a mess.
We have a joke that goes, "We live in tin."

But still we have more fun than we do wrong.
We take a simple pleasure from the rain.

HIS SLIGHTLY LONGER STORY SONG

She was older, say, thirty-five or so,
And I was eighteen, maybe. She was dark
And musical, I thought, out of a book
I hadn't read, Louisiana slow,
A chance to get my ass shot off or grow
Up quickly, outdistancing the nervous pack
Of boys I ran with. I was green but trick
By trick she taught where innocence could go
When what I wanted happened. Innocence
Or ignorance? Or neither one? Or both?
She claimed she'd taken sweetness from my life.

She cried, imagining the pretty wife
I'd hammer with some grief. She said the breath
Of love—this kind—was mostly arrogance.
She'd drink and then she'd dance
Alone and naked to the radio.
She said I was her baby. I said no.
She said in time I'd throw
Away her memory. I knew she lied.
I said I loved her body, loved her pride.

THE TRAVELLING PICKER'S PRAYER AND DREAM

Lord, forgive our drinking. Forgive our dreams
Of decency we can't shake off. Sisters
Are involved, and mothers, say our screams
That wake the whole bus up, and ministers
We come from haven't helped.

The poor are moral
But none of us have rotten teeth. Our teeth
Are good, washed by salt water. Fancy coral
Grows and forms what's called a barrier reef—
But what we're up against we can't be sure

Unless it is the sea, and the sea's too big
To drink to, and the sea's also impure
As Eve's mouth on the apple or Adam's fig.
Lord, a picker's dreams should not be cursed.
Remember the souls in the last hard town we blessed.

I WRITE IN A PECULIAR MOOD UNWORTHY
OF THE TRUST

Everybody in this house I love,
All of you, I know you memorized
And hold your faces.
Soon I'll claim I strove
To raise you not exactly victimized
And hope you live at least ninety years
With normal minds and understanding hearts—
Bruun, Kathleen, Eric, Joan, Philip,
Edward, Ruth, observe the strict defeats
A father suffers.

Your father is a tulip,
A withdrawn man who won't outgrow his fears
Of pleasant husbandry and ignorance.
Learn to avoid his awkward mental dance.

He's liliaceous to a fault. Say that
He fumbled daily in the words for it.

A BETTER THAN AVERAGE BOY RECONSIDERS THE FACT THAT HIS MOMMA TAUGHT HIM RIGHT FROM WRONG

She did—also the chilly sweats of lust—
Although how she was sensitive was nice,
For Momma's pain was real and learned and blessed.
When Momma hugged you once, she hugged you twice.

And only criminals would say these things.
I qualify. I've done time on the farm,
Six months of decent work and sweet bird songs.
The guard just hit me once to break my arm.

Hey hey hey—and now I'm going straight
Because I love my wife and family.
Friend, I keep her off the boys and hate
Myself when I'm too soft on daughter. I

Would rather be unlike my daddy, Lord.
He was a good man. Momma called him good.

FOR BERRYMAN

Considering how casually his doom
Gets off, considering all the sweats, Fuck it
Comes to mind. A fellow builds his room
And voices natural enough to fit
The insane time he does, then takes a dive . . .

Piss on the butcherman, piss on the suet
Tied in winter sacks. Birds are alive
But Big John isn't and every head has got

Its rat.
        He's company for Mistress Anne—
Who fed on now feeds the cruellest scholarship
While every lover fiddles with his chin—
Reasoning, we call for booze, the whip
To make our shitty bodies right. God damn!

No one will soon rise up like Berryman.

FOR GEN

A nuptial mass was what we couldn't do
Since I was from the Presbyterians
And you a daughter of the Irish nuns
In Yazoo City.

Loss was always true
For us—the postcard of the scourged Jesus you carried
The day we met—the case for rectitude
I'd buried in a tonk. For years we tried
For virtues we were taught, and then we married.

Children—Lord, we've born children like a pope
In spite of every secular device,
Including three at once. Wife, we are dated—
Love, these years we have excessively mated,
Though not for God. Notice the wink of Christ
So naturally the body is our hope.

WHAT THE CHANCERY JUDGE TOLD
THE YOUNG LAWYER AFTER A LONG DAY IN COURT

Name the widows and divorcees you know,
Then recollect their comments on the dead
Or gone they speak of when the lights are low.
Lord, that their memories of love are sad.
Lord, how the simple sky is always blue
And the spring grass green, while the poor marriage bed
Grows colorless, because no love stays true.
Friend, they want their sex back bad and red.

Men and women share relief sometimes,
Especially when their serious hopes break out—
We learn all evidence is ruined dreams—
We find most things are proved outside our court.

Her husband never drank a day of work.
We knew all day her time was bleak, Christ, bleak.

A BRIEF REVIEW OF *THE DEVILS*

Brueghel's wheels outside Chirico's walls
And lots of bad sex inside. It's quite a story
Although quite simple—plague is clearly glory
And the convent gleams with fancy shower tiles
Not unlike a modern locker room.

Jesus! the ample pain the eye can stand—
Lopped limbs, the eternal whipping of the big gland—
It's all about a natural man, his doom—
Bye, bye, blackbird, and the nun has an icon neck—
Louis and the Cardinal are weird
And funny. Their Power is unafraid
To kill a city for Real Politik.

It's obvious. There's one straight dick in town:
Break his bones, burn his ass, bring him down.

AFTER HAVING READ ALOUD SOME FAVORITE
POEMS THE LOCAL CIRCUIT JUDGE
ENJOYS FINE TABLE WHISKEY AND HIGH TALK

Those who fall down because of law and love,
The proper indiscretions of our race,
I'll praise and justify. Old sin will thrive
On what I say, remembering her face,
And laugh at how we always were so fancy—
In fact, had Calvin's spies caught us on film
They would have cut their eyes and called it filthy.

White people suffer a peculiar carnal dream.
White educated people suffer love
In the old way, whatever that way is.

She and I while fucking sometimes strove
To understand the loving of the ages.
Our joining recollected history.
Five times in four sweet days we both went free.

WHEREIN THE LAWYER FROM GEORGE COUNTY
RECOUNTS EVENTS SOON AND SOME TIME
AFTER HE CROSSED THE BAR

1

Red is naturally a bourbon man—
In fact the best I've known to shake a fifth
Of green Jack riding
The semi-tropical backroads of George
The summer Tucker won the D.A. race
And say, "Watch out for the higher altitudes—
They make the whiskey work too goddamned well."

The head-on chicken farm was on the rise
In George, where if the rain blows from the south
You sink completely in the Gulf of Mexico.

2

We drove and drank all afternoon the day
That Tucker won his race
Because politically he was our man—
We shot some cans before we left Red's place,
Then passed by all the ponds and creeks in George
That hold the rusting John Deere tractor parts.

Even after Red has got it shaken
Sometimes it's hard to drink it straight in George.

Tucker was our man
And he would surely win.

3

It wasn't bourbon that caused the two of us
To bury tractor parts
The afternoon the hurricane came through—
The wind and rain beat inland from the Gulf
And drowning tractor parts

I learned some strange law
On the same roads we drove when Tucker won.

It was your gin that Red went crazy on
The night the storm came through. Pressure
Made him steal those tractors from the John Deere man.

4
I got a call from Betty saying Red
Was sitting on the biggest one at dawn—
I better come on home with my new law
And reason with her man
Who wasn't often reckless with their life.

I did. I said confess. Return it all—
Though Red had by that time ruined one—
He'd torn it down to parts and nuts and bolts
And said confession never helped a thief
In George: "*This* is not your killing. *I'm a thief!*"

5
And he was right. I took to wrenches, mad
As hell to realize the hurricane
Was bending trees like switches at the brake.
Also, the Sheriff wasn't anybody's fool.
Tear the damn things down! Fill the truck!
We did. Our hands got bloody in the rain—
Though the rain was how we got the time to work
Against the law.
Red shook his Jack and drove
While I threw tractors part by part into the water.

6

We got it done in time, then faced the Sheriff
Where the water poured across the road.
He had his side and we had ours.
He said we had the tractors—
We said we never did—
But he was pissed enough to try to ford
Which got him swept away
And drowned at Little's Dam
Down from the chicken farm.
Red dove three times, recovered him, and cried for days.

7

I still see Red in dreams
Cold sober with the Sheriff by one arm—
He's yelling and waving me out of the pickup's bed—
And I still hear illegal wind like pain
Alive in every pine.

We worked to save the Sheriff where he lay
Until the water reached to pull us in . . .

It's on election day we drive the roads
Drunk to fancy tractor parts beneath
Low water lost in ponds and lost at Little's Dam.

THE LEFLORE COUNTY LAWYER
RECOLLECTS HIS CLIENT SULLIVAN

He chose that dynamite
Because the war was why she loved on him—
She loved to hear about those quilted coats
The Chinese soldiers wore—
And she went wild in split-row cotton fields.
He said she'd run off toward the brake butt-naked
Yelling she's on fire for all of him.

He never questioned her vitality
Or her smooth skin and lovely yellow hair
He followed over all those slick dance floors.
Cascades and beer bubbles and little lights
Eased his memories
Of winters in a cold Korean trench.
Garters and hose and split briefs
Hid the dark side of what she had to have
And what he gave for a long time before
He realized how sick and wrong it was.

My client Sullivan
Knelt at the edge of the woods
With those sticks of dynamite
Spread out around his boots
And studied the house he'd worked to build for her
Exactly like a slab of marble cake
Beneath a lover's moon—
Something generally fine that rots your gums
And makes the last blond curls come falling out
Unless you mix in something normal with it.
There wasn't any reason to abuse
And abuse the body he loved.
That made him sick, but not so sick as the stories
About the ones who would.

Sullivan got to his feet—he stood straight up
And lobbed them in exactly where she was.
He wasn't confused at all
By the cries of the nightbirds
Or the fog that rose from the slough.
Those explosions tore it down—those five
Explosions gave her a final perfect beating
While clapboard and glass flew around like popcorn.
He did exactly what he had to do.

THE CURIOUS LOCAL BANKER
AFTER HAVING READ A RECENT ANTHOLOGY

Their poetry is strange and wonderful
And surely using chemicals with them
Would be a good time, fresh and fanciful,
Especially with those thin girls in a wild room
Where violent gestures wouldn't be allowed,
Although I think in fact they are afraid
The ways I am.

Dead—I see the dead
In many of the images they braid
Into their long hair. They wear the fine bones
Of mad grandmothers, wear the skins of aunts
As if they know what skin and bones will mean.
They wear their poems the way brokers wore hats
Before the culture changed. But that's O.K.
Everybody means to die at play.

HAVING GAINED SOME SPIRITUAL RUTHLESSNESS
BUT STILL CONFUSED BY WHAT HAS HAPPENED
A LOCAL MAN CONSIDERS A FRIEND
WHO DIED ALONE

He was a vain man and died courageously,
Except calling him vain defines the fault
As less than what it was. I've come to see,
Now he's in the ground, how he never meant

Much more than entertainment by the love
He gave us all. His death makes love a word
To be confused by. Mean, he had to prove
Our sympathy alone. His solitude

Toward the end was fancy cruelty—
His wife, his children and his friends shut out,
He would achieve the full catastrophe,
As sailors faced where Ocean Sea must quit.

Busy in the torn rigging of his heart,
He died, I hope, in a calm mortal sweat.

HE LISTENS TO HIS BROTHER BEGIN TO ENJOY
A BEAUTIFUL SOCIAL WOMAN AT A PARTY

My brother's voice is very close to mine—
It rumbles from a baritone to a bass
Then hits the high notes in a country song.
Older, I almost hear without disgrace
Our nervousness inside all heavy talk.

I stand to hear myself bend to a lie
When a social woman ranges from the track
Our wilderness allows. (I've heard him cry
Out of confusion many nights at home
A long, long time ago.) He has regained

Composure in the thicket of her dream.
He turns a line that's absolutely charmed.
He likes the sound of her. He hardly falters.
At best we sing exactly like our father.

SOME BETTER THAN AVERAGE ADVICE ABOUT WRITING
FROM THE ELDER LOCAL NOVELIST
WHO IS A CRAFTSMAN OF SORTS
AND WISE AND PROLIFIC

Some other subjects lie around, but fear
And overcoming fear are favorites—
Especially the overcoming. Hear
The nervous ventricle. Count up the nights

Courageous lovers live through during years
Of marriage and their children. Victories
Over the foul mouth, drink and idle tears
Out of the 19th Century will please

Your decent readers. Make him catch his breath.
Then make her pull the covers to her chin.
Readers who read in bed do not love death.
Good readers like their stories almost clean.

Your books dropped to the floor, they touch each other—
You've written well enough to make them bother.

A LOCAL CONTRACTOR FLEES
HIS WINTER TROUBLE
AND SAVES SOME LIVES
IN A KNOXVILLE MOTEL ROOM

Nobody is dead yet and won't be. Right.
Right. Right. Because I am a snake aware
Of wintertime. Out there is a hard night
To study, friends, deciding I'm still fair
Enough to keep the Remington locked up.
My dreams are bloodier than movies, buddy,
Because I'm wise enough to hide the clip.
You should be sainted when you quit on ready.

Mother is gone, dead as an animal,
And Daddy is strange—he fishes in the rain—
And my ex-wife, men, will defeat you all.
Everybody longs for where they began
Or where they've never been, you better believe.
You better believe we all end up alone.

THE COUNTRY MUSIC STAR BEGINS HIS POLITICS

There are no deadlier Americas
Than those I see from stages where I work,
And over coffee in the bad cafes,
Which is how everyone is going broke
Investing in good times and sentiment
Which pays my wages.
                            Squandering their love
The size of death and a revival tent
A troubled pride is what I have to give.

Whatever else they want they hardly say,
And I don't either. I am paid to strum
And make up songs that help grown children play.
The thing I do has prospered and gone wrong.
Lord, we are multiplied and we mean well.
There's murder in the darkness I can't kill.

LONG TOUR:
THE COUNTRY MUSIC STAR EXPLAINS WHY
HE PUT OFF THE BUS AND FIRED
A GOOD LEAD GUITAR IN WEST TEXAS

The day I put him off the sun outside
The cafe window didn't have a mind
For anything but lighting up a road
Covered with hair and plates and guts and blood
Of animals. He always counted them.
In the jump seat he'd count the creatures dead
Three hundred miles until we'd stop at noon.
He'd add them up in a notebook he carried.
He said that eggs were almost perfect food.
He said he'd met the man that ate the toad.
His breakfast stories went from fair to bad:
A couple wanted children, tried and tried,
But they got fur and nails like little wings
And every time the little baby died:
Then once again they tried
While making love to all our pretty songs —
She gave her man a watch, he gave her rings,
And God forgave their wrongs,
And it was born alive, a nine-pound eye.
I fired him for that. And he was good.

FOR OUR FIFTEENTH ANNIVERSARY

I'm here for the duration, Lord,
In a big house with seven children—
Bless this place
And shower sensuality upon
The adults in it.
We have been in love five times
These fifteen years, a good marriage

And shower sensuality upon
Our children as they come of age—
Teach us to live with what they know—
Point out right times for perfect rage—
Sons, daughters, let them grow.

And thank you for the company of Gen,
So calm in bed, so often fun.

A RECENTLY RECORDED PICKER EXPERIENCES
A COMPLICATED SADNESS AND PROVOKES HIMSELF
INTO A PRAYER
for Carl Launius

There's pleasure in success. God knows there is.
For like the good man said, "Success is Salvation"—

Savage beyond repair or otherwise,
There is a ballad song, for sure, some creation
That tells exactly how awful things are—
True. There are songs and there are story songs
Similar to the cold lungs of a star.
A poor boy needs the very thing he sings.

Hidy ho—Hidy ho—the dead
In Nashville kill the virtue that we do—
Salvation, Lord, is growing in my head,
And I am frightened, Lord, to find what's new.

I saw a country woman yesterday
Whose throat was gone, whose features were all clay.

PAY ATTENTION, SON
for Tom Royals and Sarge West

The things I've said were meant for praise
And I certainly never called you a liar.
All I did say was
It isn't possible in fact
To knock down flying animals
With a cotton boll—
And don't describe trajectories
Again. It's a damned good story,
Maybe the sort we have to have
To survive—
But it never happened—
And I know your daddy is stone deaf
And I'm sure it is his true belief
His word is all that killed that dog
Your mother spotted on the ridge—
I know that dog was killing chickens
And maybe did come howling in
To die without much blood. Maybe
It did flop down and die at his feet—
And I know he didn't see or hear
Your brother fire from the porch
At the same time
He slapped his old hat across his knee
And demanded, yes, in a voice to break
The meanest heart,
Death from the beast.
I'm sure he's positive that age
Has blessed him with a final power.
All I said was I don't believe
Your brother ever hit a dog
With a 22 at 500 yards
And I'll be glad to tell him to his face.
He missed or fell short.

THE ALABAMA MAN
REMEMBERS ALL HE CAN
ABOUT THE BATTERED CHILDREN
AND THE WOMAN WITH ALMOST PERFECT SKIN
IN MOBILE SEVEN YEARS AGO

Mostly the fat one remains inside my head
Because he was most bloody of them all
And was afflicted in his mind.
                    My dread
Of what his people mean is terrible.

A damaged sister beat upon the door
I was involved behind.
                  Forgive me, Lord,
Those children crying got me off the floor
Whereon sweet love had almost shot us dead.

Continuing—I'm there for normal sin
With a woman with almost perfect skin.
She said, "We'll drive them to Emergency,"
Who were no kin to her or kin to me.

Above the pines the simple moon was bright.
After they were stitched, we said goodnight.

TROUBLED IN A DALLAS HOTEL ROOM
HE REMEMBERS LADY YEARS LATER

1

Lady—that fine old religious name
    suggesting the late whimperings of birdcall
    across the August cotton fields
    and the vague lace of nylon panties
    known on the moonlit seventh green
    of moist grass at the Rosedale Country Club—
Lady—Lady—
    you were so excellent in the blankets of humid morning
    or to be exact, false dawn
    and a long time after Rufus sang
    "Danny Boy" for the last time
    crying until our souls were warm and dark
    rolling on the moonlit seventh green
    (O dangerous banner, O strange device)—
So why within kind memory should I rebuke your gifts and
        graces?

The tolerant river stars
    have never judged you poorly—
But then of course the river stars make fools
    and the weather was awful the next day.

2

All that afternoon the sun fell in
    your momma's gin drink at poolside—
Your momma kept on saying
    I think I mostly love summer because of
    these gindrinks out here at poolside—
Except I'm fairly sure she said *boo-sad.*

Boo-sad! I feared the meaning of boo-sad.

Insight comes hard
      in summer lawn chairs at boo-sad
      with those fine old gindrinks in your hand—
      with the glistering heat roiling ghostly
      over the poisoned cotton fields—
And in that boiled twilight, a spectre,
My living father among the waves saying
      They all end up like their mothers, Son—
      study her mother close, Son.

And alas though you, Lady, were thin then
      as a strand of kudzu vine from a high tree,
Your momma wasn't.
                              She was a pear
With the big end turned up
      with toothpick legs that finally quit
      in thick feet she'd stuck in cherry sandals.

She kept on saying she was fond of me
      because *most boys these days and times*
      are raised thoughtless and basically wrong
      and haven't got whole afternoons
      to simmer a little drunkenly out here at boo-sad
      with me and Lady and Daddy.

3
I wanted to believe you favored Daddy
      who listened to grand opera
      and loved money and Tennyson
      and flying his Piper Apache under the Greenville bridge
      with your new friends, including me—
Because any man who loves to dive his plane to just above
      the fiery river—*pointillé* sun from Arkansas—
      intoning *Maud* until he's passed beneath the thing—
Can't be all bad, nor can his daughter.

A LOCAL MAN CAN'T HANDLE THE LADY'S PROBLEMS

Lady, I'd rather face my worse faults
Ten times in one day,
Even how I break out on friends
And those dreams of mine that kerosene
The neighbors' cats,
Than listen to your son's fears
And how you hate your husband.
I'm selfish. They weaken me.

After how he can't keep his food down
And after how your old cock with a pelt
Like a puma's is shacked up with his typist in the mountains,
God, I suck on my lips for hours—
I stare down my own boy's body and see my wife there.

Lady, I can't give you what you want.
I will not reason
Backwards through your life,
My little wisdoms sweating from each pore
And every convolution of my brain
A trough for small-time modern lecheries—
You're beautiful—
Go away.

TRYING TO EXPLAIN A BAD MAN TO A GOOD MAN AT THE NESHOBA COUNTY FAIR IN 1971

Just because he fights dogs
And got in on the famous murders
Doesn't mean he'll kill you if
You walk up to his orange face and say
You're all hide and cruel inside and out.

He might just listen for where you come from.
He might just have his daddy's political sense
And say for a fact you Delta men
Lost power fifty years ago.

He might just twist an eye up and say
The niggers are riding you boys now,
And if you shunt or say something nervous,
Then, he might, at just that point,
Assault your body and break your face.

VISIONARY OKLAHOMA SUNDAY BEER
for Clarence Hall and Jane Cooper

The small window opened. I asked for the six-pack
I paid for, then saw the women playing pool
In the loud and common light where ball and stick
Have always met.

              The oldest on a high stool

Was big as a mound but wasn't simply fat.
She glistened and shouted—she was having fun
With all the other Indians—each one great
With child in a way to make that bulb a sun.

All fancy with no men around, they played.
Hey, let me in is what I think I said.
I meant of course to ask where are your men
And what of pageantry and life and death?

Her break shook me and a brown arm closed down
A show I would have stayed a season with.

DEALING WITH MARY FLETCHER

1

Bolton Howard never served his time
Or anything. But he was strictly gifted
At dancing on a bill—
And thick as any pig he had three wives
Who if the word is right
Never saw him naked
And never wanted to.
He started with a ruined pulpwood truck
And once he wrecked his car and killed his child
By Mary Fletcher. He cried but didn't drink,
Which is insane,
Then sold his trailer park and went to hell.

2

After Mary Fletcher everything
Is pale, the story goes,
But no one gives details.
I used to watch her study clothes she bought
As if they might be fancy groceries.
She never tanned, for all the sun she took,
Who was as sensitive as gardening.
She married twice
And had good friends who always kept their tongues
Except to shudder when her name came up.
They never smiled.
I saw her buy three summer dresses once.

3

Hugo Lafayette Black
Once praised the legal mind of Albert Fletcher.
Judge Fletcher's opinions were written carefully
And his hedges were high as a goal
Because his troubled wife, a Methodist,
Was given to public tears for little reason—

And they never practiced anywhere but here,
And he raised his daughter almost by himself.
His wife before she died
Wrote a classic work on evidence
He took no credit for.
He wore a Panama and thick glasses.

4

I think all history
Revolves around my wife
Who says my head is like a ball of twine
I rarely use,
Or tape I lick until I gag. Her eyes
Are careless after life
But comforting in love,
And when I talk too much she won't put out.
Howard and the Fletchers piss her off.
I give her flowers twice a year, a brick
For Valentine's.
I give it in a sack.

5

Sometimes confusion in a private sorrow
Breaks a man. Davis is precisely that.
He was Mary's friend
But never came to much,
Considering the money he started with,
And Tulane Medical
And then a Jackson practice up until
Her child was killed. Connections are obscure.
He fell apart—
He lost his steady hand
Except for tying flies. He does that well
And writes pulp novels by another name.

A LOCAL MAN PONDERS A LETTER
HE HAS RECEIVED
FROM A LIBERAL WOMAN
HE CONTINUES TO ADMIRE
for John Little

She writes to say I am a radical,
Writing cursive, stretching her long mad hand
Straight up and down in such a way to fill
One yellow page torn from a legal pad.
She says my root is better than my tree—
Deep living root but very little trunk,
No complicated leaves, no canopy
Creating shades for squab and pleasant drink.

God knows exactly what the woman means.
Picnics? She writes I am a radical.
Lord, she is lovely, she is fed on dreams
And one time praised my green convertible.

Also, she says I am a sober mole—
No brilliant bird—I am a mole, a root.

A LOCAL MAN ESTIMATES WHAT HE DID FOR HIS BROTHER WHO BECAME A POET AND WHAT HIS BROTHER DID FOR HIM

I shot the chicken in the tree above
Where Herbert stood howling after I'd shot.
Bitterly he cried so loud of feathers Love
Itself became involved. Lord, lord, the fit
He threw was terrible. He said his head—
His sacred head—was daubed for poetry—
He said my cruelty would make him mad—
He said it was a ritual catastrophe.

Herbert was splattered with old chicken blood
And pink feathers from eyes to knees. He said
Later, twelve years later, that he was sad
He'd frightened me. Within a month he died.
On his deathbed he reached out for my hand
And said we come from where we get the wound.

SOME LOCAL MEN AFTER THEIR ELECTION
for President Jimmy Carter

They are suspicious now in the strange air
The morning after election. They are troubled
And sobering, afraid of their first beer.
They are responsible—they know they've gathered
Responsibility. Of this they're sure.
And they know responsibility is work.

They think of work and then they think of war.
They're less afraid and swallow their first drink,
Which isn't beer, is whisky. They're not broke.
Their new responsibility is good

And different and possibly no trick.
By now it's possible they're not too bad—
It is possible to be responsible
Away from war and the more terrible.

POETRY FROM ILLINOIS

History Is Your Own Heartbeat
Michael S. Harper (1971)

The Foreclosure
Richard Emil Braun (1972)

The Scrawny Sonnets and Other Narratives
Robert Bagg (1973)

The Creation Frame
Phyllis Thompson (1973)

To All Appearances: Poems New and Selected
Josephine Miles (1974)

Nightmare Begins Responsibility
Michael S. Harper (1975)

The Black Hawk Songs
Michael Borich (1975)

The Wichita Poems
Michael Van Walleghen (1975)

Cumberland Station
Dave Smith (1977)

Tracking
Virginia R. Terris (1977)

Poems of the Two Worlds
Frederick Morgan (1977)

Images of Kin: New and Selected Poems
Michael S. Harper (1977)

On Earth As It Is
Dan Masterson (1978)

Riversongs
Michael Anania (1978)

Goshawk, Antelope
Dave Smith (1979)

Death Mother and Other Poems
Frederick Morgan (1979)

Coming to Terms
Josephine Miles (1979)

Local Men
James Whitehead (1979)